CreativeKiDs
publishing

Copyright © 2005 Creative Kids Publishing, a division of
Transglobal Communications Group Inc.
Edmonton, Canada T5S 1V8

The Great Treasure Adventure

Bobby Beaver was diving down into the water, when he saw something sparkling down at the bottom of the pond. He carried it up to the surface.

"What's that?" Billy Jo Bunny asked.

"A bottle with paper in it," Bobby said. He climbed up on the dock and carefully pulled the old paper out.

"Looks like a map," said Benson.

"A treasure map!" Billy Jo blurted out.

Henry Hedgehog had just arrived when he heard Billy Jo and grabbed the paper from Bobby's hands.

"Hey!" Bobby protested.

Henry examined the map. "This will be a cinch to find. Let's go," he said.

"Maybe we should ask Rosey," Sherry Squirrel suggested.

"What for? It won't take long with me in charge," said Henry.

Henry was older and seemed to know his way around. Everyone followed him to a large hollow log.

"Looks like the right spot," said Billy Jo.

"I don't think we should go much further," Sherry worried.

"It's not far," Henry assured, but he really wasn't sure at all. His young friends followed him into a part of the forest they had never been before.

They walked and walked until they came to a big stone.

"This must be it," Bobby said.

Billy Jo looked at the map in Henry's hands. "You sure this is the right stone, Henry?"

"Of course I'm sure," Henry shot back.

"Nothing else looks the same," Sherry said. "We're supposed to turn right at the rock, but there's no path."

"It's probably just overgrown," said Henry. "The pond, where the treasure is, must be just up ahead."

Sherry looked at all the unfamiliar trees. "We're lost!" she suddenly cried.

"Henry knows where we're going, right Henry?" Benson asked.

"You don't know, do you?" Billy Jo said crossly.

"I'm pretty sure we're close," Henry answered sheepishly.

"You got us lost!" Sherry exclaimed.

Henry had gotten his friends into this mess and he'd have to find a way out. "If only there was a way for someone to see where we are," he said.

Then, Henry had an idea. "Sherry, do you think you could take this map to the top of the tallest tree? It'll be like a flag and signal to others where we are."

Sherry looked up at the towering tree. "I can do it," she said confidently, and took the treasure map in her mouth. From branch to branch Sherry climbed up the tall tree. Then, very carefully, she stuck the map on the very top and ran back down.

The friends sat and waited together. Finally, they heard the flutter of wings.

"Rosey!" they all rejoiced.

"How did you get all the way out here?" Rosey asked.

"We were following a treasure map. I got us lost," Henry admitted.

"But now you're found—thanks to your paper flag," Rosey said.

They followed Rosey through the forest. By the time they reached home, they were all very hungry and very tired.

The next day at the pond, Old Blue asked them about the map, "Did it have a hollow log on it?"

"How did you know?" Benson asked.

"I made that map when I was just a pup. Over there is the hollow log," he replied.

"Oh! That hollow log!" Henry cried.

"Then, where's the treasure?" Bobby asked.

"Right here," Old Blue patted an old board on the pier he was sitting on.